MW00807611

For Willa,

Who's a beautiful
part of nature's designs! ♡

Love,

Mrs. Rikki Zoey and
Ruthie Darling

Keep on Reading

MRS. LIBRA
AND
ZOEY ZEBRA

Love, Pops !!

BY
RUTHIE DARLING

ILLUSTRATED BY
ADAM DEVANEY

ARK Publishers

PRINTED IN THE U.S.A.

MRS. LIBRA
AND
ZOEY ZEBRA

BY
RUTHIE DARLING

ILLUSTRATED BY
ADAM DEVANEY

COPYRIGHT © 2017 RUTHIE DARLING

All rights reserved. No part of this book may be reproduced, stored in a retrieval system, or transmitted in any form or by any means, electronic, mechanical, photocopying, recording or otherwise, without the prior consent of the publisher.

GASSNER, RUTHIE
DARLING, RUTHIE
KRITZIK-GASSNER, RUTH

1ST EDITION
FIRST PRINTING
ISBN: 978-0-692-90086-4

LIBRARY OF CONGRESS CONTROL NUMBER: 2017938453

ARK Publishers
Palm Desert, CA 92260

www.ruthiedarling.com

ruthiedarling8@aol.com

Dedicated to children and adults – everywhere:

We are all *a small part of Nature's designs!*

- R.D.

Mrs. Libra lived in a zoo,

with Zoey, her daughter, who was just over two…

And at just over two Zoey wanted more lines,

o she could change her facial designs.

She tried to move the stripes on her face,

but when she was done they were in the same place.

"How do I move my black stripes around?"

she wondered aloud as she sat on the ground.

Then came the day when she heaved a big sigh,

and crawled under a fence which she thought was quite high

"Where are you going?" Mrs. Libra called out,

"You're sure to get lost as you're roaming about!"

"I'm looking for stripes to put on my face,

and I think they might be in some faraway place...

Cause I've looked in the bushes and I've looked all around,

and I haven't found even one stripe on the ground.

I've also tried looking in beautiful trees,
but all that I've found were some striped honeybees!"

So Mrs. Libra snuck out of the zoo,

to go with her daughter who was just over two.

Her mom wasn't sure if black stripes could grow,

but to tell you the truth she just did not know...

So they went into town and walked into a store,

but the stripes that they found were
black stripes on the floor.

Next, they went to a store that sold stringy, black candy,

and were given this candy which they thought was just dandy...

But when she stuck the candy right next to her nose,

it fell on the ground landing near a red rose.

When she saw a striped scarf she could
e on her head,

he thought, "This could fall off while I
sleep in my bed!"

Next, they went to a store that sold all kinds of paint,
but the smell of the paint almost made Zoey faint...

So they left the paint store and sat under a tree,
and dear Zoey looked at a stripe on her knee.

She rubbed that black stripe but it just stayed right there,

and as hard as she rubbed it would not disappear.

"If I can't change the stripes on my body or face, maybe, just maybe, they're in the right place!"

As they sat together under the tree,
the mom looked at Zoey and said
with great glee...

The stripes that you have are in the right place,
ncluding the ones that you have on your face.

You need to be happy with the way that you look,

and it's not what you see in some kind of a book!"

Since nothing else was left to do,

Mrs. Libra and Zoey returned to the zoo.

Zoey had learned a great lesson that day,
as she and her mom had gone on their way.

Zoey had learned to be proud of her lines,

which are only **a small part of Nature's designs!**

Questions:

How many main types
of zebras are there?

What color is a zebra
when it is born?

What color is a zebra's skin?

Where do zebras live?

What do zebras eat?

Can you find the worm?

What have you learned
from this story?

About the Author

Ruthie Darling, author of "THE HOLE STORY" and "MIRANDA THE PANDA" is a former Elementary School teacher who has been inspired by children throughout her life. Her newest book, "MRS. LIBRA AND ZOEY ZEBRA," is a charming story about learning to accept and appreciate yourself for whom you are. It is brilliantly illustrated by **Adam Devaney** and it is to Adam that she owes her everlasting thanks and appreciation for making Zoey and her mother, Mrs. Libra, come alive!

HER MISSION: *Empowering children and adults through the world of children's literature!*

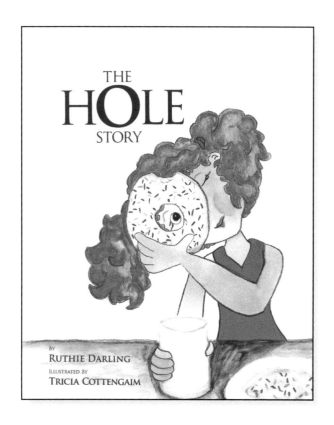

THE
H**O**LE
STORY

BY
RUTHIE DARLING
ILLUSTRATED BY
TRICIA COTTENGAIM

MIRANDA THE PANDA

BY RUTHIE DARLING
ILLUSTRATED BY TRICIA CAPRARO

Also available from
ARK Publishers

ruthiedarling8@aol.com

www.ruthiedarling.com

CPSIA information can be obtained
at www.ICGtesting.com
Printed in the USA
BVHW020854300919
559643BV00016B/11/P